Rockets

MRS MAGIC

Circle Magic

Wendy Smith

A & C Black • London

KT-555-978

for Richard

Rockets

MRS MAGIC – Wendy Smith

Circle Magic
Crazy Magic
Magic Hotel
Mouse Magic

First paperback published 2000
First published 2000 in hardback by
A & C Black (Publishers) Ltd
35 Bedford Row, London WC1R 4JH

Copyright © 2000 Wendy Smith

The right of Wendy Smith to be identified as author
and illustrator of this work has been asserted by
her in accordance with the Copyright, Designs
and Patents Act 1988.

ISBN 0-7136-5332-9

A CIP catalogue record for this book is available
from the British Library.

All rights reserved. No part of this publication may
be reproduced in any form or by any means - graphic,
electronic or mechanical, including photocopying,
recording, taping or information storage and retrieval
systems - without the prior permission in writing of
the publishers.

Printed and bound by G. Z. Printek, Bilbao, Spain.

Chapter One

Mrs Magic ran the Black Bat Hotel.

Puss and Partridge helped run
the hotel.

While Puss and Partridge busied themselves getting the hotel ready for the big day...

Mrs Magic spoke to the big black crows...

and left a note for the hotel rats.

She was decorating Moon Dog Hall with fresh webs when Puss tore in.

Mrs Magic went to greet her new guests.

One by one the magicians were whooshed to their rooms.

Chapter Two

The young magicians soon settled in.

The young magicians were very
excited when Mrs Magic explained
the programme for the weekend.

Puss had made some posters
for the show.

Partridge showed everyone where the show was to take place.

And after a light supper, everyone climbed to the hotel tower to watch the arrival of the Wacky Wizard.

Through the starry midnight sky the Wacky Wizard appeared in a spectacular display of broom work.

The Night Rider

The Sweep

The Broom Glider

The 'Look no hands!'

The free-fall broom swoop

That wizard's nuts.

Chapter Three

All day Saturday the young magicians practised their tricks with a little help from Mrs Magic.

Cherry made rabbits pop out of a hat beautifully.

Dave the Wunda made lemonade flow like a fountain.

Melvin the Marvel made a hamburger disappear.

Now you see it.

Now you don't.

Spot on.

Trev and Kev spun plates together at exactly the same time.

Puss and Partridge were most impressed.

They decided to go into town and
do a bit of advertising.

See the Wacky Wizard.
See youngsters
Turn into
Young stars.

boom
boom

Tonight's the
night for
stars and
magic.
The famous
Wacky Wizard
will do his
sawing-in-two
act.

jingle
jingle

And all the while everyone else was so busy, the Wacky Wizard just put up his feet and did nothing.

Mrs Magic was concerned.

As Puss and Partridge were still in town, Mrs Magic arranged the Wacky Wizard's table herself.

Chapter Four

Puss and Partridge had done such a wonderful job advertising the show that a huge crowd had arrived.

The young magicians were feeling nervous enough, and when they saw how full Moon Dog Hall was they felt very nervous indeed.

Puss did a spell and made them feel better.

And before they knew it the Wacky Wizard was standing at the foot of the stage. The show had begun.

Rachel, Dave the Wunda, Kev and Trev, Cherry and Melvin the Marvel, all came on stage to perform their tricks.

Rachel and her Indian rope trick.

Dave the Wunda with his Ace of Hearts card.

Cherry and her rabbits.

plate spinning

Kev

Melvin the Marvel with his silk hankies

plate spinning

Trev

The audience loved the
young magicians.

But the fact was they had really come to see the Wacky Wizard. They cheered wildly when he came to do his star turn.

Charlie got up and climbed on stage.

The Wacky Wizard brought up the
sides of his magic table and took
up his saw.

The audience gasped as the Wacky Wizard began sawing Charlie in half.

In a great puff of smoke the Wacky
Wizard made the final cut.

But when the smoke died down it
was clear there was only one half of
Charlie left.

Chapter Five

As you may imagine, Mrs Magic drew
the curtains at once, and Partridge
put on the interval music.

The young magicians searched high
and low for Charlie's other half.

On the other side of the curtains the
audience was growing restless.

Mrs Magic decided to invent a new
spell to bring back Charlie.
Puss swept back the curtains.

We are delighted
to bring you
our very own
star turn,
Mrs Magic.

From beyond the moon
in a flash,
from the sea of stars
you'll see,
In a wink of an eye,
The other half of our
lucky boy Charlie.

In a shower of stars the two halves of
Charlie were united, much to the
audience's great delight.

The Wacky Wizard was not at all delighted.

And in a fit of revenge he rang the local paper.

Long after the audience had gone home, the reporter from the Daily Moon came to see what was going on.

Chapter Six

The story broke the very next day.

DAILY MOON

1ST

STRANGE GOINGS ON AT THE BLACK BAT HOTEL

Brave wizard reveals how ½ boy goes missing in Witch's Magic Weekend. 'I was shocked', said Mr. Wacky.

At the local police station P.C. Winder was having his tea on the early shift.

Partridge and Mrs Magic were happily preparing breakfast for the young magicians when the police arrived.

At that very moment, the Wacky Wizard was creeping up to the Tower to fly off. Puss spotted him through the window and called the young magicians.

Thanks to Rachel's Indian rope trick the Wacky Wizard did not get away.

45

When she heard the news that her jewellery had been recovered, Lady Mountfitchett invited the young magicians to perform at her lovely home, Mountfitchett Castle. There was a splendid party afterwards.